D0923193

DAFFY DUCK
Space Creature

story by Gina Ingoglia
pictures by Darrell Baker

A WHITMAN BOOK
Western Publishing Company, Inc.
Racine, Wisconsin

"With a little luck, I'll be in time for breakfast," said Daffy Duck as he rang Elmer Fudd's doorbell. "I hope this is his morning for waffles!"

Daffy waited a minute, then rang the bell again. "How *can* he be out when I'm so hungry?" he muttered.

Then he heard Elmer's voice coming from the backyard.

"Woo! Woo!" Daffy shouted happily. "Breakfast, after all!"

As he walked along the side of the house, he heard Bugs Bunny, Porky Pig, and Petunia talking.

"Let's have our picnic tomorrow," Petunia suggested.

"That's a great idea!" exclaimed Porky. "I'll help make sandwiches, and I'll bring some grape juice, too."

"I'll bring carrots," Bugs promised.

"And *I*," Elmer announced proudly, "will make my famous chocolate fudge cake."

"Oh, that sounds good," Daffy said to himself. "I could eat it all right this minute." He was about to join his friends and invite himself to the picnic, when he heard something else.

"Someone should tell Daffy," Porky said.

"I don't know why," Petunia protested. "Daffy never brings food to our picnics. He just grabs everybody else's food, then eats more than anyone!"

"You're right," Bugs agreed. "He's a nice duck, but he *is* a little bit greedy."

Daffy couldn't believe what his friends were saying! Sadly, without ever being seen, he turned around and walked away.

Daffy wasn't unhappy for long, however. By afternoon, he had an idea: He would bring *fun* instead of food to the picnic! He hurried to the city dump and sorted through the trash. "Oh, this is perfect," he chuckled, picking up a piece of old garden hose. He tossed it on his pile of other junk.

At the picnic the next day, everyone had plenty to eat. Petunia poured grape juice, Bugs passed the carrots, and Elmer cut huge pieces of cake.

When they had finished their lunch, Bugs suggested a game of softball. "Petunia can pitch, Porky can bat, I'll catch, and Elmer can play outfield."

"Oh, no!" Elmer cried. "I won't chase that ball awound all by myself!"

"We really should have two fielders," said Porky. "It's too bad Daffy isn't here. He's a great fielder."

"I wish we had invited him," Petunia said. "He always can think of something fun to do."

At that moment, they heard a strange hornlike sound.

Honkity-honk, honkity-honk.

"What was that?" asked Petunia.

The sound came again: *Honkity-honk, honkity-honk.*

Elmer pointed. "Wook! It's something in the twee!"

Down from the tree fluttered a strange-looking creature.

"Watch out, doc!" said Bugs, jumping out of the way. "Here it comes!"

"Good afternoon, Earth people," said the creature. "I have come to visit."

"A space creature!" Porky exclaimed.

"You speak English vewy well," Elmer said.

"I studied hard," said the creature. Looking at the food on the table, he asked, "What are you doing?"

"We're having a picnic, doc," Bugs explained. "That's spelled P-I-C-N-I-C."

"How nice," said the creature. "And what are those?"

"Sandwiches," said Petunia. "Would you like one? We have just finished eating."

The creature gobbled up one sandwich, and then he ate seven more. "UMM-ummm, delicious!" he exclaimed.

"Here, twy this," said Elmer. "It's gwape juice, and it's dewicious, too."

"And you'll like Elmer's cake," said Bugs. "C-A-K-E."

"Is *cake* as good as *sandwich?*" asked the creature. He took a bite. "Oh, this is very good!" He greedily grabbed another piece.

"You Earth people have wonderful food,"
he said after he had eaten every last crumb.
"Thank you for sharing with me."

With a funny little bow to the group, he
flew away over the treetops.

Honkity-honk, honkity-honk.

"Well, that certainly was unusual!" Petunia exclaimed.

"He had an unusual appetite, too," said Bugs. "I'm surprised he could take off after eating all that food!"

"I'm glad he came, though," said Porky. "Nothing much was happening before he arrived."

"Nothing else is very likely to happen, either," Petunia added. "We might as well go home."

As they were packing up to leave the park, they heard a familiar voice.

"It's Daffy!" exclaimed Elmer. "Say, guess what, Daffy! We saw a space cweature! He came to our picnic!"

"He was a hungry creature, too," Bugs added. "Too bad he didn't leave anything for you."

"Think nothing of it," said Daffy. He patted his full tummy, then looked at Elmer's empty picnic basket. "Your cake was delicious, Elmer. *Honkity-honk, honkity-honk.*"

"Daffy!" laughed Petunia. "It was you! You were the space creature!"

"Yes," said Daffy. "I heard you planning the picnic at Elmer's. I also heard those nasty things you said about me."

"We're sowwy if we hurt your feewings," said Elmer. "You weally are our fwiend."

"Yes," said Porky. "The picnic wasn't much fun until you came."

"Now that we're all here," said Bugs, "how about a quick game of softball? Daffy, you can play outfield."

"I'm sorry, Bugs," said Daffy, "but I can't. I ate too much at the picnic. That's P-I-C-N-I-C." With a final little *honkity-honk*, he lay down to take a nap.